SAM'S JUST SAM

LINDA MORSE
ILLUSTRATED BY PAT PRESCOTT

Bear Hug Press

For a single copy of this book, please contact:
Bear Hug Press
111 Stark Hwy. So.
Dunbarton, N.H. 03046
(603) 774-7811
BearHugPress@aol.com

Book design and production by:
The Floating Gallery
331 West 57th Street, #465
New York, NY 10019
(212) 399-1961   www.thefloatinggallery.com

Linda Morse
Sam's Just Sam

1. Author 2. Title 3. Children's Literature 4. Picture Book
Library of Congress Catalog Card Number: 2001 135631
ISBN 0-9713567-0-X Hardcover

SAM'S JUST SAM

This book is dedicated to:

Sam's pal Bill
and Sam's 'little' brother Ben;

Sam's godparents and his friends, especially those from
DES and SRS, and all special needs children,
their families and friends;

and to Pat, whose pictures capture the spirit of the boy.

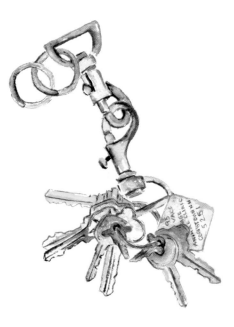

Sam sat up, wide awake. He picked up a huge wad of gum from the nightstand, popped it into his mouth, and hopped out of bed.

Moonlight shone on the other bed
where Ben, Sam's little brother, was fast
asleep under a pile of stuffed animals.
Sam grabbed his favorite blanket and
left the room.

Turning the hall light on, Sam thumped happily and noisily down the stairs. He turned on the television. Popping in his favorite video, he grabbed two pencils and began drumming on the sofa and lampshade in time to the music. There were lots of dents in the lampshade.

Upstairs, Sam's parents heard the noise. "The lampshade is a cymbal again," said Mom, sleepily.

"Yeah. The rhythm sure is great, though," mumbled Dad, still half asleep. He and Mom admired their son's drumming skills and understood the endless energy that was part of what made Sam so special.

Yawning, Mom got out of bed. As she went down the stairs, she heard the refrigerator door slam and Sam drumming on the ice cream box with a spoon as he skipped back to the TV room.

Sam greeted his Mom at the bottom of the stairs. "Oh, hi, Mom!" Sam's smile went from ear to ear as he gave her a big bear hug.

"Morning, Sam," Mom smiled in return as she hugged Sam. "Please put the ice cream away, and I'll make breakfast." She was used to Sam's unusual early morning snacks, but she didn't mind because he always ate a good breakfast anyway.

"Oh, all right," Sam said reluctantly as he and Mom headed for the kitchen. And then, in the slow, halting way that Sam talked, he asked the same question he asked every day. "Mom? I . . . do have . . . school . . . right?"

"Yup," Mom said.

"Yeeaa!" Sam whooped with excitement and raced back upstairs to his bedroom to get dressed, accidentally bumping into Ben on the stairs.

"Sam, DON'T!" Ben yelled. Ben had just awakened and was still a little sleepy.

"Oh! Sor . . . ry, Ben . . . ny!" called Sam from the top of the stairs. Ben headed for the TV room, more awake now.

In his room, Sam whipped off his pajamas and tossed them straight into the air. They landed somewhere near his bed. He yanked his shirt over his head, pulled on his jeans, and grabbed his favorite possession, a key ring full of keys. Nine keys and one dog tag hung on the key ring. The keys didn't unlock anything, but Sam loved to hang them on his pants and hear the jangling sound they made when he walked. He would take them off and get help with putting them back on several times during the day.

Back downstairs, Sam's Dad was waking up with a cup of coffee in the kitchen. Sam handed him the keys.

"I can't . . . put these on. Could you . . . put these . . . on my pants? Please?" Sam asked.

"Sure." Dad hooked the key ring onto Sam's belt loop, smiling as he thought about how special the keys were to Sam. As Sam sat down to eat breakfast, Dad asked, "So, Sam, what's our phone number?" Sam's teachers had been working on helping Sam remember important information. Sam thought a minute.

"528 . . . 6 . . . 7 . . . 1111?" he said.

"No. That's too many numbers. It's 528-6711," Dad replied, a little disappointed.

"Oh, darn!" Sam exclaimed.

After breakfast, Sam grabbed his jacket and backpack. He stored the huge wad of gum next to the milk in the fridge. Dad grabbed his coffee cup, and they both headed for the door to meet the school bus.

"Bye Mom, bye Ben. I'll sss . . . see you . . . this after . . . noon!" Sam's keys jangled noisily as he walked. Straightening up the kitchen, Mom sighed when she noticed the size of the gum in the fridge. Sam adored his gum, but she worried about him choking. She cut it in half.

At school the children got ready to start the day. Sam walked up to his teacher and grinned at her.

"Good morning, Sam!" she said, returning his smile. And then she leaned toward him and asked softly, "Hey Sam, What's your phone number?"

Sam thought a minute. "528 . . . 6771?"

"Almost, Sam! 6711. Good try." replied his teacher.

The school day began with writing exercises. Sam eagerly raised his hand and almost jumped out of his chair whenever his teacher asked a question, even though he often didn't know the answer. His enthusiasm made schoolwork more fun for his classmates and teachers.

Learning was harder for Sam than for his classmates. His endless energy made him want to get up and walk around rather than sit and think. That was just the way Sam was.

After lunch Sam and his classmates headed for the gym. When Sam got there, he began stomping his feet, enjoying the loud noise that echoed in the gym. He laughed, whooped and made all kinds of funny sounds, even raspberries.

The kids lined up and practiced shooting hoops. Sam was a natural athlete. He was quick and could jump higher and run faster than many of his classmates.

The kids divided into two teams and played a quick basketball game. Sam caught a pass. He dribbled the ball towards the basket, paused and tossed it. The ball swished through the hoop.

"Yesss!" he yelled.

A minute later, at the other end of the court, Sam's friend Drew shot a basket.

"Nice shot, Drew!" Sam called. Sam always cheered for both sides at ball games. His friends smiled when they heard Sam cheer them on.

When gym was over, Sam noticed his friend Laura walking slowly back to the classroom by herself, looking at the floor. Sam went over to her. He peered at her face, smiling, but concerned.

Laura looked at him and said, "I missed every basket today."

"Ohhh, it's OK," Sam said softly, giving her a big bear hug. Laura smiled at him, instantly feeling better.

Computer time was next. Although talking and understanding words were hard for Sam, computers were easy.

"Sam, I can't do this. Can you help?" called Michelle, one of Sam's classmates. She couldn't find her favorite spelling game on the computer.

"Sure!" said Sam. He tapped the keyboard quickly and in a few seconds, Michelle saw the game pop up on the screen. "Thanks, Sam," she said, grinning.

Then the school day ended. Sam and his friends climbed into their buses and headed for home. When the bus stopped at Sam's house, his dog Topper bounded up the driveway towards him, panting happily. He had been sitting in the front yard waiting patiently for the school bus to stop.

"Hey, Top!" shouted Sam, giving the big golden retriever a hug.

Sam ran into the house. He grabbed his gum from the fridge.

"Need more gum," he muttered to himself, looking in a kitchen drawer. The phone rang, and Sam picked it up. "H . . . H . . . Hel . . . lo?" he said.

"I've got it, Sam," Dad said through the phone in the shop. Sam hung up the phone and thought about his phone number. "528-67 . . . oh phooey."

He shrugged his shoulders and went back outside.

Sam was on the front yard hitting golf balls effortlessly with his club when Mom and Ben drove down the driveway, home for the day. Once, Sam had hit a ball through a window, but Mom was only a little mad.

"Hi Mom, hi Ben!" Sam called, dropping his golf club and running over to the car, Topper at his heels. He gave them both a huge bear hug. Mom and Ben walked into the house to start supper.

Sam went back to hitting golf balls again. Suddenly, a stray dog appeared on the driveway. Right away, Topper ran toward the dog, barking, and the two dogs ran towards the road.

"TOPPER!" Sam yelled. But Topper kept going. He ran after the dog, and Sam ran after Topper.

The stray dog, Topper, and Sam ran out of the driveway and onto the street. Cars slowed down, the drivers wondering what was happening. The stray dog, Topper, and Sam kept going, running along the side of the road.

Finally, a long way from home, the stray dog ran into the woods. Topper and Sam stopped, out of breath. Sam looked around, but didn't know where he was.

"Are you lost?" called a man raking leaves. "What's your name?"

At first Sam didn't say a word, then blurted out "528-6711!"

The man smiled, nodded, and said, "Come off the road, and I'll be right back!"

Sam and Topper walked into the man's driveway and waited for him to come back out of his house.

"Your Mom's on her way," he said, smiling.

A few minutes later, Mom's car pulled up beside them. Sam and Topper hopped into the car as Mom thanked the man. Mom didn't say a word to Sam as they drove home.

Back home, Mom and Dad sat Sam down and talked very seriously to him. Ben listened, too.

"Sam, don't ever, EVER follow Topper away from our house like that again!" Dad said in a quiet, stern voice. "Come tell us if he runs away," Mom added. She looked closely at Sam. "Deal?"

Sam nodded. His shoulders rounded and he tried hard not to cry. It was Ben's turn to give Sam a big bear hug.

"Oh, it's OK Sam," Ben said. Sam smiled and hugged Ben back.

Smiling now, Dad said, "Hey Sam, Mom and I are VERY proud of you for remembering your phone number! Good job!"

And Sam grinned from ear to ear.

The day had been an exciting one for Sam. During supper he grew sleepy, so the boys got ready for bed right after eating. Knowing Sam would soon fall asleep, Mom tucked him in first.

"You still my special big boy?" she said, giving him a kiss. She made sure both boys went to bed feeling good about themselves.

"Yep!" said Sam, giving his Mom a smile and big hug.

Mom went to Ben's bed and gave him a kiss. "And are you my special little boy?" she asked him.

"I'm NOT little!" Ben protested. Unlike Sam, Ben had no trouble saying what he thought.

"Oops. Are you my special boy?" she tried again.

"Uh huh!" Ben snuggled under the covers with his stuffed animals.

"Good night, Ben. Good night, Sam."

"'Night, Mom," Ben said.

Sam didn't reply. He was already sound asleep,
tucked under the covers with his favorite blanket.

And on the nightstand sat a ring full of keys and a
huge wad of gum.